THINGS
I Can Make

Sabine Lohf

You can make all the
things in this book!

Chronicle Books • San Francisco

EDITOR'S NOTE: Younger children should only undertake these projects under adult supervision. Parents and teachers should match crafts to the appropriate skill level of the child.

First published in the United States in 1994 by Chronicle Books.
Copyright © 1994 by Ravensburger Buchverlag Otto Maier GmbH, Germany
All rights reserved.
Printed in Hong Kong.
ISBN 0-8118-0667-7

CIP Data Available.

Distributed in Canada by Raincoast Books
8680 Cambie Street, Vancouver, B.C. V6P 6M9

10 9 8 7 6 5 4 3

Chronicle Books
275 Fifth Street
San Francisco, CA 94103

Table of Contents

BEADS

BOXES

BUTTONS

CLOTH

CORKS

A Cork Train • Cork Castles • A Zoo
Cat and Mouse Game • Floating Animals • Parachutists
Flying Elf Game • Ink Stamps • A Desert Oasis

LEAVES

Leaf Printing • Leaf Animals • Leaf Cards
Grass Dolls • A Flower Crown • Leaf Collage
Leaf Jewelry • Leaf People

PAPER

Crumpled Paper Pictures • Torn Paper Collage
Animals Cards • Stars and Snowflakes • Peek-A-Boo Theater
Animal Racers • Accordion Animals • Masks • Windmills

STONES

Painted Stones • Stone Animals • Racing Ladybugs
Aquariums • A Stone Family • A Fish of a Different Color
Mosaic Boxes • Stone Castle

Sparkling Bead Fish

By gluing beads into a shell, you can make a special gift.

Or, you can pin the beads onto a piece of cardboard, cork, or styrofoam, to make a pretty wall hanging.

Bead Weaving

1. Knot the end of your thread to one side of the loom threads. String your thread with beads. You should have one less bead than there are threads on the loom. Run the beads underneath the loom threads.

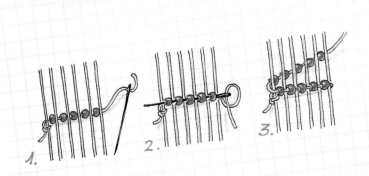

1.
2.
3.

So, that's how it's done!

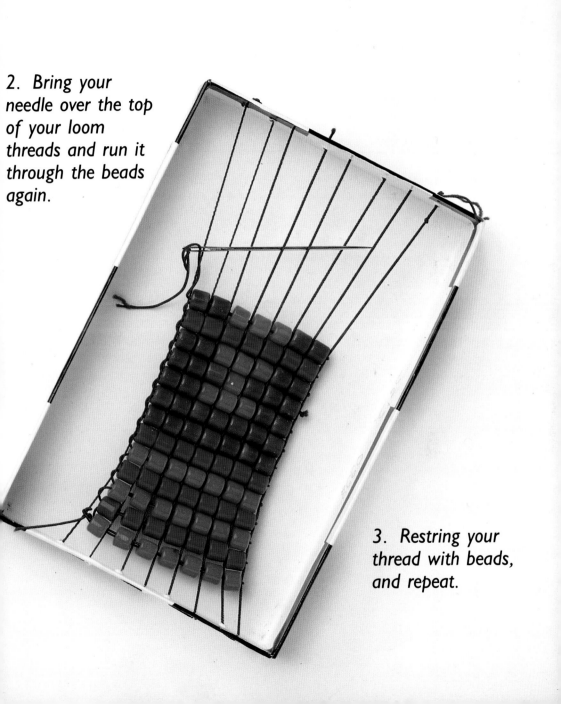

2. Bring your needle over the top of your loom threads and run it through the beads again.

3. Restring your thread with beads, and repeat.

A Beaded Marionette

You can collect feathers to make a fuzzy hen.

Look, she can dance!

1.

2.

3.

4.

5.

Fold a piece of
colored paper
to make a
pouch for
catching beads.

Hey, that looks
like fun!

Bead Toys

Bead Instruments

You can make drumsticks by taking two wooden sticks and gluing a large bead on the top of each one.

Now you're ready to perform!

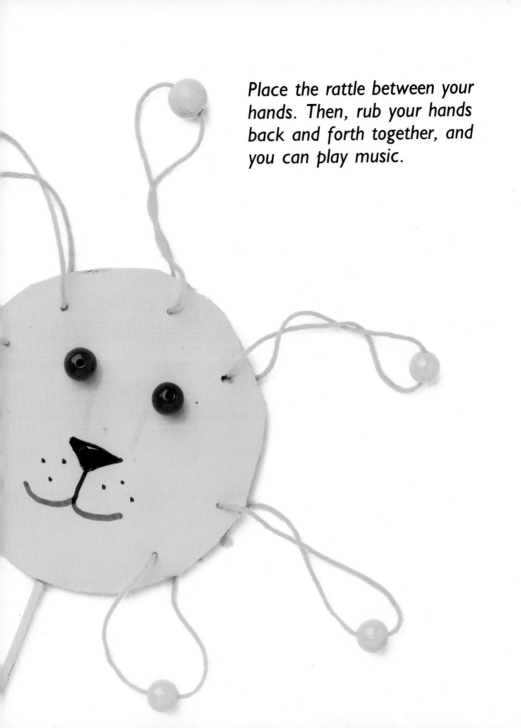

Place the rattle between your hands. Then, rub your hands back and forth together, and you can play music.

Bead Key Rings

Bead Ghosts

Bead Gardens

With a little imagination, you can grow a beautiful bead garden.

Box Train

Finger Puppets

Start by making a small hole, just big enough for your finger, in the bottom of a box. Then, use paints or construction paper to make a face for your puppet. You can hide behind a sheet and give all your friends a real puppet show!

Hi, boys and girls!

Magic Boxes

Surprise!

You can keep all your props in a little trick box.

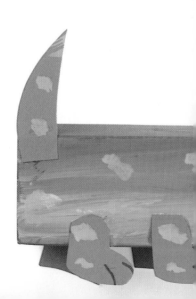

Abracadabra!
It's snowing at the beach!

This crocodile has a long tongue!
(Secret: a long piece of string is
hidden inside its mouth. When you
pull on the string, it keeps growing
and growing.)

Box Ships

Puppet Theater

What a good show!

1. First, take a piece of cardboard or construction paper and fold it into two square boxes. Then, cut out a large hole from one of the boxes and place it on top.

2. Cut out the curtains from some old cloth and glue them on either side of your stage.

3. After painting your puppets on paper, cut out the shapes and glue them onto a stick. Now you are ready to place them backstage.

First, glue the duck and water onto a strip of cardboard. Then, when you place a piece of clear plastic over the duck, you can move the stick and it will look like the duck is really swimming.

Box Friends

Hush.
The baby is sleeping.

A Box Camera

Before you start, paste your picture inside the camera so you will be ready for your subject. Now, aim and shoot! After you've taken the picture, you can remove your photograph and say, "Look, it's you!"

Button Animals

Button pictures

Button Jewelry

Use string or leather or ribbon to thread a necklace.

I'm also going to make a bracelet and a ring.

Button Collage

I'm going to glue this butterfly onto this shiny paper.

The leaves are glued on. The apples are sewn on.

Button-Toss

Use buttons as
tiddlywinks, or simply
toss them onto the
scoreboard, and see
who can score the
most points.

Button Puppets

Button Wheels

Add a sail, and you have a sailboat.

A papertowel tube makes a great race car!

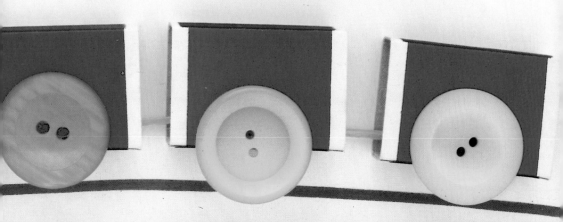

Button Garden

ADEMAS EXTRA
Suerdieck S. A.

Loom Weaving

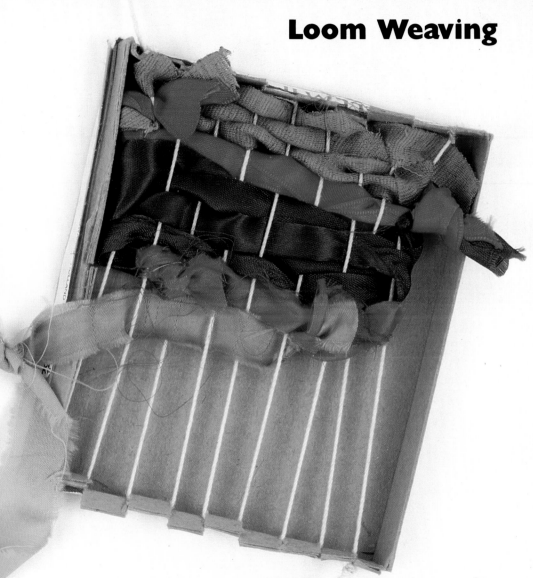

Cut cloth into strips. Then tie or glue strips together. Cut a row of slits an inch or so deep in the ends of a cardboard box. Stretch string from one side of the box to the other. You've made a loom!

Painting

Hmm. Can you think of anything my picture needs?

Spooky Puppet

Braids

Braid three strips of cloth.
Then use your imagination!

Flutter Ball

Stuffed Animals

Cut out felt parts. Sew or glue them together. Stuff the body with cotton and sew on buttons for eyes and nose.

Are you hungry?

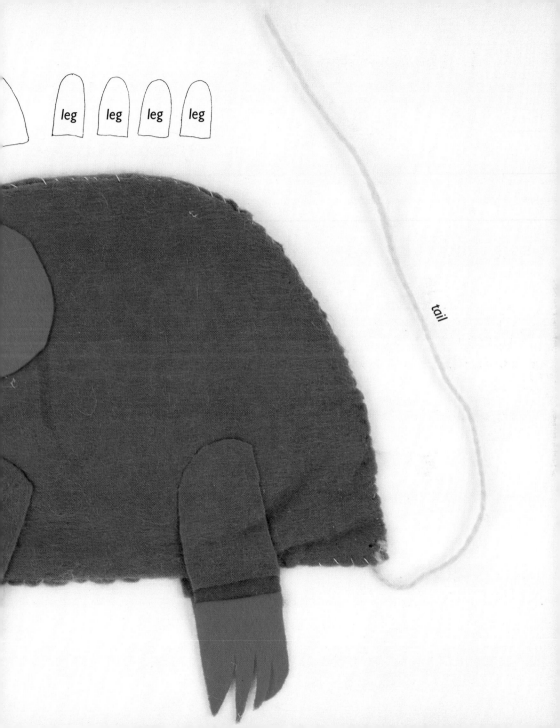

leg leg leg leg

tail

Finger Puppets

Cut felt strips. Wrap them around your finger and glue or sew them together. Glue on eyes and mouth, etc.

finger puppet

Step right up and listen to my story about the Lion, the Elf and the Frog-King!

hand puppet

Collage

Cork Castles

A Zoo

Hello, up there!

Cat and Mouse Game

Rules for playing:

Each player places a mouse on the board and holds the mouse by its tail. When the cat (a player who tries to cover the mice with a bowl) appears, the mice are quickly pulled back, away from the circle. The mice that get trapped are out of the game. The player whose mouse stays on the board the longest is the winner and gets to be the cat in the next round.

Look out!
Here comes the cat!

Floating Animals

Cut out a paper figure and stick it into a cork that's been cut in half.

Is there room for one more?

Parachutists

Look out below!

Glue the strings onto tissue paper.

The parachute is rolled up like this before it is thrown high into the air.

Flying Elf Game

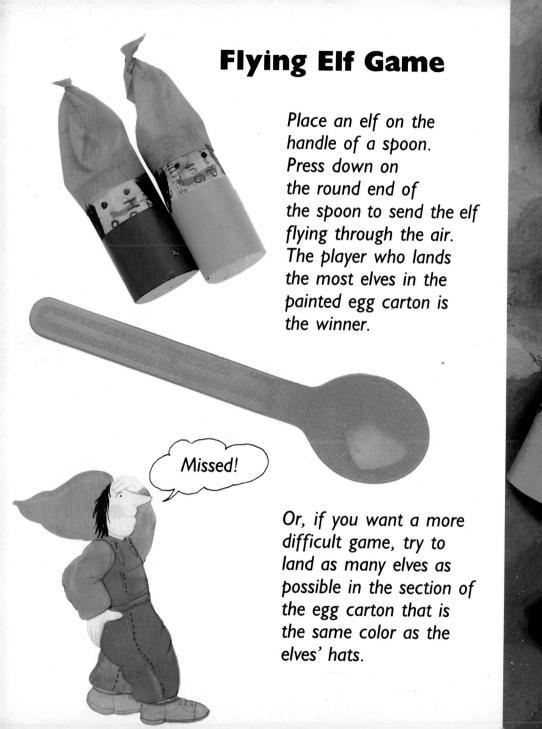

Place an elf on the handle of a spoon. Press down on the round end of the spoon to send the elf flying through the air. The player who lands the most elves in the painted egg carton is the winner.

Missed!

Or, if you want a more difficult game, try to land as many elves as possible in the section of the egg carton that is the same color as the elves' hats.

Ink Stamps

Press the corks into an ink pad or into real paints. You can make all kinds of colorful pictures.

A Desert Oasis

Leaf Printing

Cover a fresh leaf with paint and then press onto a sheet of paper. You can make all kinds of colorful prints.

15. 9. 88

Leaf Animals

Leaf Cards

Now, that's a nice card.

Glue leaves and flowers to colored paper to make beautiful gift tags or stationery.

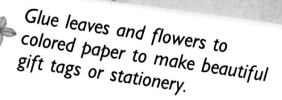

Grass Dolls

A Flower Crown

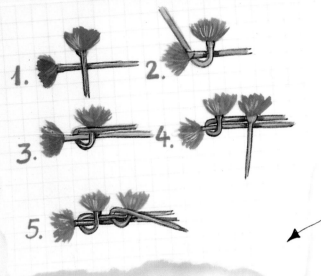

This is how to weave the flowers together.

I'll make you a crown!

Leaf Collage

Let's find a spot for you.

Leaf Jewelry

Thread leaves and berries on a strong piece of thread to make this lovely necklace.

You can also make a leaf hat.

What a well-dressed bear!

Leaf People

**Crumpled
Paper Pictures**

Torn Paper Collage

Animal Cards

Cut paper into strips.

Here comes
the wind!

Fold the strips in half.

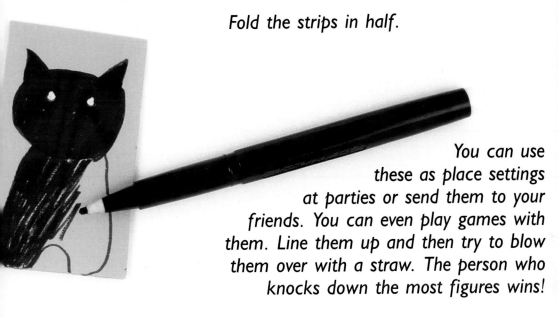

You can use
these as place settings
at parties or send them to your
friends. You can even play games with
them. Line them up and then try to blow
them over with a straw. The person who
knocks down the most figures wins!

raw animals on the cards.

Stars and Snowflakes

1. Fold a paper
   square into
   a triangle.

2. Then fold it
   again.

3. Now cut
   notches along
   the edges.

Peekaboo Theater

Take a large envelope (or two pieces of paper that have been glued together along the edges). Cut out windows and doors and slit openings along the sides and bottom of the envelope. Now you can slide figures like this in and out of the stage.

Animal Racers

Cut out legs and fasten
them to the backs of
the paper animals.

Wow! Look
at them go!

Accordion Animals

Cross paper strips over one another like this, and then fold the strips alternately backwards and forwards.

Masks

Windmills

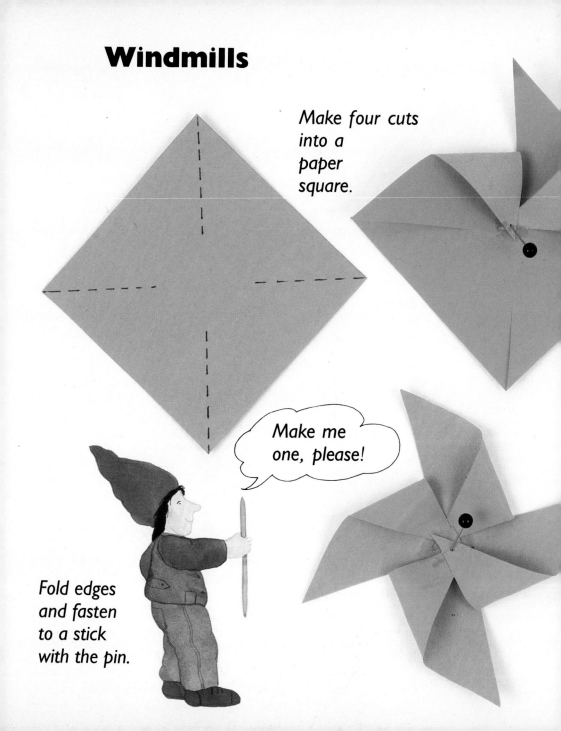

Make four cuts into a paper square.

Make me one, please!

Fold edges and fasten to a stick with the pin.

Painted Stones

You can paint letters on stones and spell your name.

You are going to have a lovely red cap!

Stone Animals

Using clay, you can make these wonderful stone animals.

Hello, goat!

Racing Ladybugs

Place a smooth piece of cardboard or paper on a slope. Each racer chooses a ladybug and places it at the top of the slope, in its own lane. The one who slides to the farthest end first, wins!

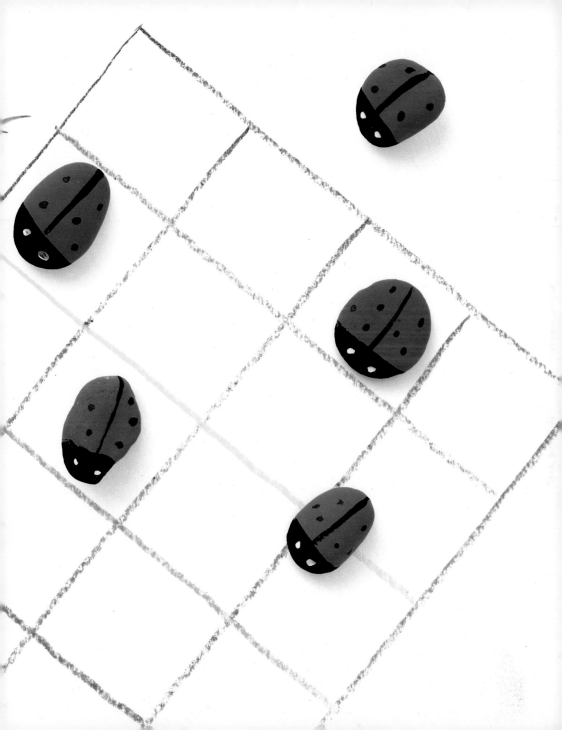

Aquariums

Would you like
to meet
some other fish?

A Stone Family

If you use your imagination, you can make all kinds of figures.

The little stone baby should sleep soundly now.

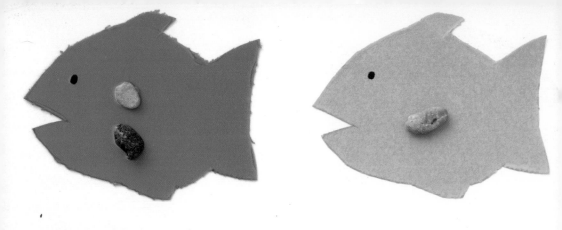

A Fish of a Different Color

First, cut several fish out of colored paper, or with chalk draw them on a large piece of cardboard or directly onto the pavement. Each player takes a turn, aiming to land the stone on a fish. The player who gets the most, wins!

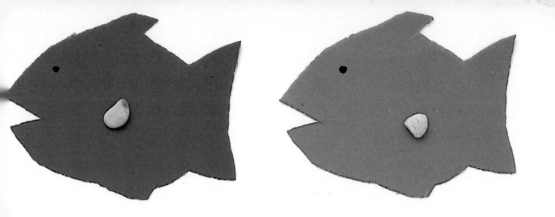

If you want an even more challenging game, paint the stones the same colors as the fish and try to land the stones on their matching fish.

Mosaic Boxes

Boxes make wonderful gifts.

I'll put this inside the box, too!

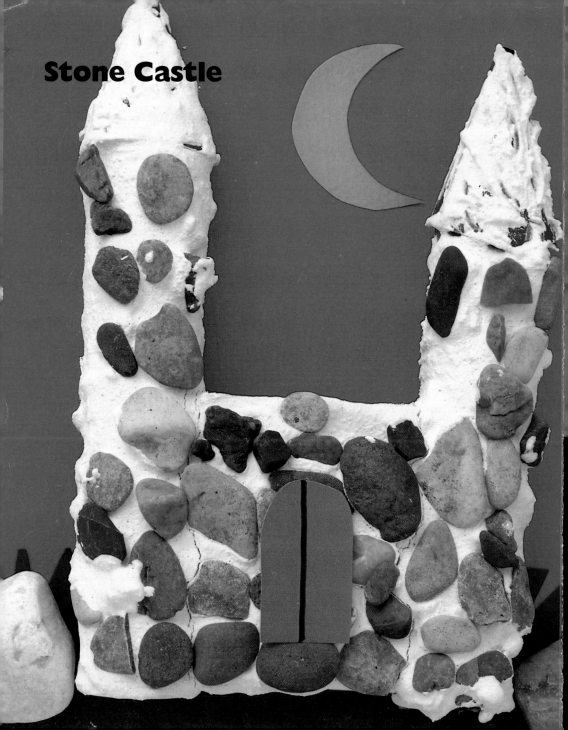

Stone Castle